For everyone who's ever found a home in the library. —J. F.

For all the wonderful librarians who share their love of books with the world. —S. L.

Henry Holt and Company, *Publishers since 1866*
Henry Holt® is a registered trademark of Macmillan Publishing Group, LLC
120 Broadway, New York, NY 10271 · mackids.com

Library of Congress Cataloging-in-Publication Data

Names: Funk, Josh, author. | Lewis, Stevie, illustrator.
Title: Where is our library? : a story of Patience and Fortitude / written by Josh Funk ; illustrated by Stevie Lewis.
Description: First edition. | New York : Henry Holt and Company, 2020. | Audience: Ages 4-8. | Audience: Grades 2-3.
Summary: Patience and Fortitude embark on a journey around New York City in search of their library's missing books.
Identifiers: LCCN 2020008868 | ISBN 978-1-250-24140-5 (hardcover)
Subjects: LCSH: New York Public Library—Juvenile fiction. | CYAC: Stories in rhyme. | New York Public Library—
    Fiction. | Libraries—Fiction. | Lion—Fiction. | New York (N.Y.)—Fiction.
Classification: LCC PZ8.3.F95926 Wh 2020 | DDC [E]—dc23
LC record available at https://lccn.loc.gov/2020008868

Our books may be purchased in bulk for promotional, educational, or business use. Please contact your local bookseller or
the Macmillan Corporate and Premium Sales Department at (800) 221-7945 ext. 5442 or
by email at MacmillanSpecialMarkets@macmillan.com.

First edition, 2020 / Design by Patrick Collins and Cindy De la Cruz
Printed in China by Hung Hing Off-set Co. Ltd., Heshan City, Guangdong Province.

10 9 8 7 6 5 4 3 2 1

42ND STREET

A Story of **Patience** & **Fortitude**

WHERE IS OUR LIBRARY?

written by

JOSH FUNK

illustrated by

STEVIE LEWIS

CLOSED

CHILDREN'S CENTER

Henry Holt and Company
New York

Just after midnight, as all New York dozed,
Silently dreaming in bed,
The last of the shops and the markets had closed,
When Fortitude lifted his head.

Patience woke, too, and the best friends agreed;
Their night was about to begin.
The library waited with stories to read.
The two eager lions crept in.

Sneaking inside was their nightly routine.
Tiptoeing to the ground floor.

But something had happened they hadn't foreseen.
And Fortitude let out a ROAR!

"The children's room looks rather different tonight,"
Patience said. "What's going on?"
Fortitude twisted his head left and right,
Then blurted, "The books are all gone!"

Fortitude gallantly rose to his feet.
"Follow me! I've got a plan!"

Hastily, both of them rushed to the street,
And hidden in shadows, they ran.

Fortitude yelled, "See the lights! Look up there!
That's where the books have been taken."
But when they arrived in the heart of Times Square,
He realized that he'd been mistaken.

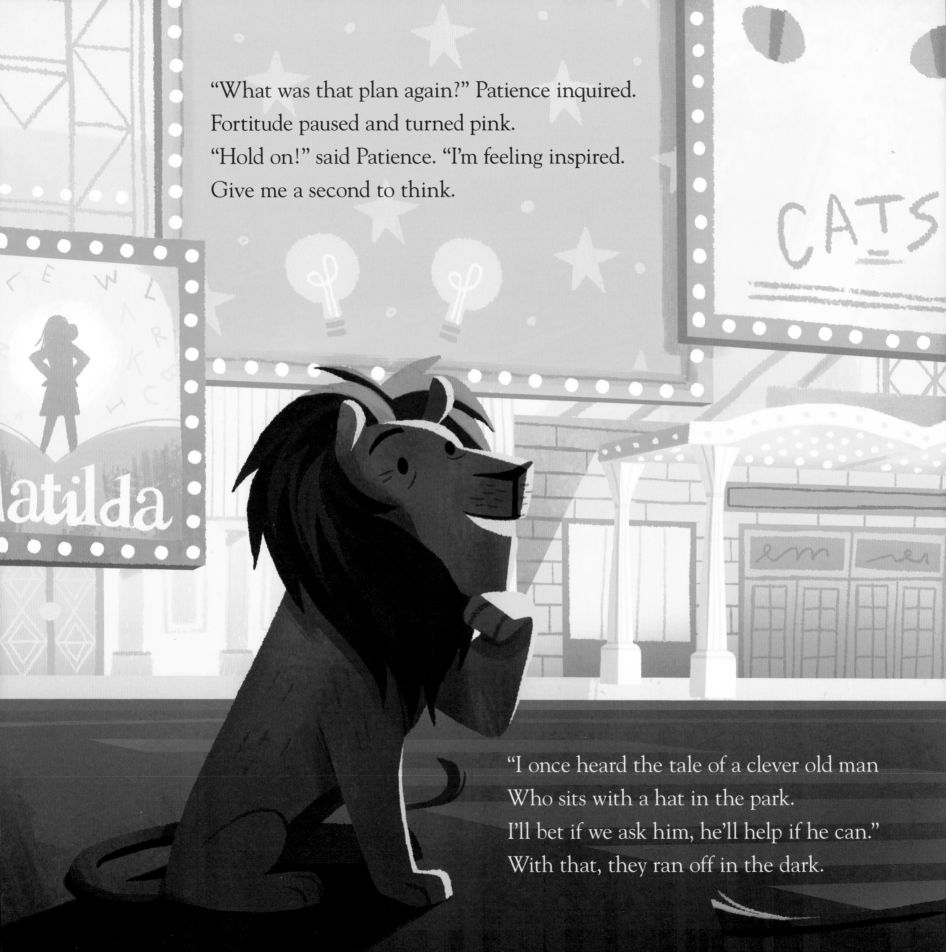

"What was that plan again?" Patience inquired.
Fortitude paused and turned pink.
"Hold on!" said Patience. "I'm feeling inspired.
Give me a second to think.

"I once heard the tale of a clever old man
Who sits with a hat in the park.
I'll bet if we ask him, he'll help if he can."
With that, they ran off in the dark.

They entered the park by some fancy hotels

And skirted a fountain or two.

Stealthy as foxes and swift as gazelles,

They scurried by Central Park Zoo.

Over a hill, by a boulder and bridge,
A carousel ride and beyond,
Down through a tunnel, then over a ridge,
The lions arrived at a pond.

Fortitude sped to a statue. "It's him—
The clever old man with the hat!"

"Indeed," said the Hatter, who straightened his brim.
"I issue a riddle, big cat:

Why is a raven akin to a desk?"
Fortitude gave a blank stare.

That's when he noticed the girl, statuesque,
Beside her a dormouse and hare.

"Ignore him," said Alice. "The wise man you need—
He sits over there with a duck."
They thanked her and dashed with a torrent of speed,
Craving a little good luck.

"Our books have gone missing!" they told the great Dane.
Hans Christian Andersen blinked.
The writer said, "Lions, I see you're in pain,"
And pulled out a quill to be inked.

☐ Washington
  Heights
☐ Harlem
☐ 96th street
☐ Bronx L. Center
☐ Hamilton Fish park
☐ Jefferson Market
☐ Chatham Square
☐ Ottendorfer
☐ Webster

"These are the library branches I'd check."
He handed the lions a list.
"Libraries?" Patience asked, twisting his neck.
"How many branches exist?"

Fortitude blurted, "There's more than just one?!"
Hans Christian Andersen grinned.
"The world is a series of miracles, son.
Now hurry and race like the wind!"

Patience and Fortitude searched many places;
Libraries came in all sizes.
Each of them held lots of old friendly faces
And always amazing surprises.

They scoured each library, scanned every stack,
And pored through each awesome collection.
They found some new books, but they wanted theirs back!
Where was *their* old children's section?

From Harlem they flew up to Washington Heights
And down to the Upper East Side.
They wandered and wondered beneath the dim lights,

In Lower Manhattan, they combed every block.
How would they find what they needed?

Fortitude roared as he looked at the clock.

"Give us more time!" Patience pleaded.

"Excuse me!" a voice from above shouted down.
"What's going on over there?"
"Our books have gone missing. We've searched the whole town,"
Said Fortitude, full of despair.

The kite dragon stated, "You need new perspective."
Patience agreed, looking north.
"A view from up high will be much more effective."
And thus the two lions set forth.

Up on the High Line, the sun now ascending,
Slowly it dawned on the two.

Their library: lost. Their quest was now ending.
They hurried back home feeling blue.

Nearing their home, only one block away,
Fortitude noticed a sign.
"Children's and Teen Center! Opens Today!"

"The old Children's Center—it seems that it's moved . . ."
Patience began to explain.
"And that's why the signs have said *new and improved!*"
Said Fortitude, stroking his mane.

Their library: found; it was safe and secure
On the opposite side of the street.
But the lions were thrilled with their city-wide tour,
For finding new worlds is a treat.

The Sights of *Where Is Our Library?*

✦ Patience and Fortitude live outside the Fifth Avenue entrance of the Stephen A. Schwarzman Building of The New York Public Library. They have perched there since 1911 and were given their names in the 1930s by Mayor Fiorello La Guardia in recognition of the qualities he felt New Yorkers would need to survive the Great Depression.

✦ Patience and Fortitude encounter the *Alice in Wonderland* statue as they make their way through Central Park. Sculpted by José de Creeft in 1959, this statue is notable because children are welcome to climb on it.

✦ The wise man with the hat whom Patience and Fortitude are looking for is the Danish children's author Hans Christian Andersen. His statue, sculpted by Georg John Lober, features Andersen's fairy tale "The Ugly Duckling" balanced on his knee. The sculpture has sat in Central Park since 1956.

✦ The lions visit the 96th Street Library, the Bronx Library Center, the Hamilton Fish Park Library, the Harlem Library, the Washington Heights Library, the Ottendorfer Library, the Jefferson Market Library, and the Chatham Square Library—all branches of the New York Public Library. With ninety-two locations, the New York Public Library is the nation's largest public library system.

✦ Look up! Patience and Fortitude meet a kite dragon at the Chatham Square Library, an encounter inspired by the book *Henry and the Kite Dragon*. Many of the New York City locations the lions visit on their library quest are also the settings for well-known books for children. Some titles that Patience and Fortitude come across on their journey include *And Tango Makes Three*; *The Curious Garden*; *Eloise*; *The Gardener*; *Herman & Rosie*; *Ida, Always*; *Lyle, Lyle, Crocodile*; *Madlenka*; *Nana in the City*; *Red & Lulu*; *Sector 7*; *Tar Beach*; and *Uptown*.

✦ Patience and Fortitude can't find their beloved Children's Center in *Where Is Our Library?* . . . because it's moved! As of autumn 2020, the New York Public Library's Children's Center is located at the newly reimagined and completely renovated Mid-Manhattan Library, which is renamed the Stavros Niarchos Foundation Library.